Cosy Burrow Books

VALKYRIE ACADEMY DRAGON ALLIANCE
Book Five

EMPOWERED

I0585543

"Kara the wingless Valkyrie's journey continues, and in this installment of the story, she sets out discover why the trickster god, Loki, would steal dragon eggs, and she finds a mysterious mentor to teach her how to control and use her magic to prove her worth and help Asgard." Susie D., Line Editor, Red Adept Editing

VALKYRIE ACADEMY DRAGON ALLIANCE BOOKS

Cosy Burrow Books

VALKYRIE ACADEMY DRAGON ALLIANCE

EMPOWERED

KATRINA COPE

Midgard ~ for your endless beauty and inspiration

GET UPDATES & NOTIFICATIONS OF GIVEAWAYS

Would you like a FREE copy of Marked?
Visit here:
https://www.katrinacopebooks.com/valkyrie-academy-dragon-alliance

Through this link you can sign up for my newsletter and receive a FREE copy of Marked plus updates about my fantasy books, sales and notification of giveaways.

- CHAPTER ONE -

The pages rustle as I flick through the book, my fingers stiff and uncertain. *This can't be right.* My mind wants to reject what I'm seeing. The need to slap myself across the face is strong. I have to prove that I'm not dreaming. After closing the cover, I stare at the front. It is a picture of Loki in his god form. The artist has portrayed him well—the pale skin contrasting with his long black leather pants and vest, and the cape that flows to his ankles. His dark hair is greased back and falling to his shoulders, accentuating his pointy nose and narrow, spirited eyes.

My eyes refuse to move away from this picture. Rarely have I seen Loki, but maybe he travels around Asgard in other forms or doesn't stay on Asgard for long. I'm not sure. He doesn't usually associate with the Valkyries, although the dragons seem to hold him in some kind of regard. Unlike the other gods of Asgard, he is able to change into dragon form and communicate with them. The dragons have trouble communicating with the other gods because of the gods' thick-headedness.

But Loki's changing into a dragon to understand them is purely an act. From what the dragons tell me, Loki is intelligent and can understand them in all forms, but they don't want the other gods, like Odin, to know that the dragons can speak to most beings directly.

I open the book to the page that holds the creature then turn to the page with the old woman, followed by the page with the girl who looks slightly younger than me and could disguise herself as a Valkyrie. They are all images of Loki. Each well-crafted image by the artist of this book is a reflection of what Loki has shifted into.

I flick back to the creature that they call a zmey and stare at it, taking in the pointy snout, the sharp teeth, the ears like a bat's, and the talons that are large yet shaped like a bird's. The short round fluffy body is a sharp contrast to the dragon-like membranous wings that protrude from the zmey's back. The zmey has given me much grief over the last few years.

As I stare at the picture of the creature, my mind swirls, trying to process the information and work things out. More recently, I have spotted the creature flying around Asgard. It attacked Heimdall the day that I broke the rules, distracting him, and I used the opportunity to enter Midgard, yet I have also run into it on several occasions. I now understand why this creature was in the area when the old woman pulled me aside to talk to me—the same woman illustrated in this book as a shape Loki shifts into. They are the same. The creature wasn't after the old woman, as I initially thought. The scar on my shoulder, which the creature gave me, tingled when I met her and the young girl. It even prickles when the creature flies over me.

I study the page with the creature, and underneath the image is a bulleted list of symptoms from the creature's scratches. My finger traces the words.

Beware of this creature.

- *It has long, sharp claws.*
- *It is shrewd like Loki.*
- *It can attack, and just because it is Loki doesn't mean it won't attack you.*

- *Beware of its scratch. If it scratches you, you have been marked with the curse of magic.*

Symptoms:

- *A sharp pain that pierces deep into the scar when you get within a certain range of this creature or other forms of Loki.*
- *Tingling combined with a strange numbing sensation running through the area of the scar and any limb attached to it.*

Be warned:

If a form of Loki touches the scar, it will increase the chances of the magic manifesting. With each contact, the magic will grow until eventually, it will explode. At first, this magic will not show. It will only manifest when emotions require it to or desperation occurs. Eventually, though, you will soon be able to demonstrate this magic at will.

Beware of this creature, as with anything to do with Loki. One must always be on guard. He is the god of mischievous intentions that do not change with whichever form he takes.

I stare at the page in disbelief. So this creature has marked me with magic, just like the old woman warned, the one that I now know is a form of Loki. He must've been seeking me out so he could touch the scar and make the magic rise to the surface. Precisely as the book describes, with each visit from one of these forms, the tingling manifested. No wonder the old woman was so keen to touch my arm.

I'm a wingless Valkyrie with no unique talents, so I don't understand why he would choose me. He could have flown away that day that I chased him off the dragon's nest and left me alone without marking me.

A tingle in my arm erupts, and I rub it absentmindedly. Perhaps the sensation has surfaced because my head is in this book and I'm thinking so hard over it that it's making me remember the scar. But then I remember what happened in the bathroom and before the fight on the top of the mountain. I gaze at my body. I still have blood and scratches from the battle all over me, and my wound is still aching and weeping. It wasn't a dream. I had used my magic—magic I didn't know I possessed and don't know how to use.

I look at my left hand—the culprit of the damage—and can see nothing special. Somehow this hand made Rota and Prima unconscious. It wasn't a dream at all. I take in all the creases and lines within the hand's shape, then hold my right hand next to it. It looks the same. Nothing has happened to the right hand, only my left. The one attached to the shoulder tarnished with the scar that was marked by the zmey. The hands are still the same color, and the lines appear the same. Yet somehow, the left hand managed to cause damage and knock some Valkyries unconscious. I have never heard of this happening before. Perhaps the elves or the fairies have this magic or have heard of a Valkyrie having it before.

Staring at my hands, I try to let it sink in, and I wonder who can help me with this. I will need training and help to discover the answers. I don't know any fairies or elves, let alone any that can help me. We are taught that they are dangerous and untrustworthy, yet I don't know anyone else to ask.

Observing the image of the creature a little longer, I curl my fingers into a fist before closing the book. Loki stares at me from the cover. He's probably the best one to ask, if I can track him down.

My chair grates across the stone floor as I push it back and stand. With the book hooked under my arm, I approach the library desk. The librarian is hunched over another book and glances up when I approach.

"Jannika, where would be the best place to find Loki?" With the cover facing up, I place the book on the bench, and it scrapes as I push it forward.

She takes in the cover of the book then eyes me with a serious expression. "If you are after Loki to discuss the contents of this book, then you're going to have a hard time. The author wrote this book because Loki is hard to track down." She grabs the book, and it scratches the surface as she spins it to face her. The front cover thuds on the bench, and the pages rustle as she flicks through them. "These are only a few of the shapes that the author knows Loki has represented. Loki will only be found when he wants to be found." Her mouth tweaks at the corner. "He will often take on one of these forms. However, he has many other shapes, making it almost impossible to find him. Especially if he thinks you know of this book."

"Would he be around the palace?" I watch as she flicks through the pages.

She glances up and smiles, her eyes full of understanding. "If Loki was there in god form,

9

don't you think you would have seen him while you were lurking around the palace?"

"Oh, I don't lurk around the palace."

She peers at me, arching an eyebrow.

"I only visited there briefly to rescue my dragon." The words tumble out of my mouth.

The eyebrow drops. "Yes, I know. That was my point. I know that you have upset Odin and he wishes you harm, or to have you locked up in the dungeons."

"Is that all anybody knows?" I let out a frustrated sigh, and my shoulders slump. "Doesn't anybody know about the good things I've done?" I push back from the bench and take a deep breath. "Besides, the things I did— like stealing my dragon back—was to follow the agreement of the alliance. Odin is not supposed to hold her."

She closes the cover of the book with a soft thud. "Yes. But what Odin is supposed to do and what Odin wants can often be two very different things. Just be careful. And I doubt you will find Loki there, so don't go putting yourself at risk to find him."

"Thank you."

"Go get this cleaned up." She indicates the bloody and torn patches of leather on my body.

- CHAPTER TWO -

I reach for my side and look down at my clothes. The librarian is right. I need to see the healer and get cleaned up. My wound is healing slowly, but it is best to check that it's not infected. After the unfairness they displayed in the battle, it wouldn't surprise me if the winged Valkyries contaminated their blades. I should also check on Hildr and Eir to see if they're okay.

My leather pants squeak as I wander down the hallway, and my mind is overloaded with all the information I have learned from the book. It is hard to process it all, especially when mixed with what the dark elf has told me. It is shocking to learn Loki is involved, and I can't imagine why a god would mark me then pursue me afterward.

I want to run to the palace and demand to speak with Loki, but as Jannika said, he's probably not there, and I'm not convinced that Odin won't arrest me. He told Eingana, the leader of the dragons, that he wouldn't touch me, but he often changes his mind. I'm eager to find Loki and see if he will fill me in on what is going on.

As I glance at one of the flickering sconces on the wall, it hits me—Loki is the one stealing eggs. Apparently, the zmey is still taking the eggs from the dragon wastelands. If the book is correct, then the dragons mustn't know the creature is Loki, or else their trust would shatter. The dragons are using Loki as a translator for Odin. *Is he betraying them to Odin?* If he is taking their eggs, he must be betraying them.

The knowledge torments me. I don't know if I should tell the dragons that it was Loki who tried to steal the dragon's eggs. If they find out it is Loki, then this may make them distrust the Asgardians more. It may also ruin my relationship with them. But then again, it might ruin my relationship with them if they find out that I know and didn't tell them. A whirlwind builds in my stomach, and I clutch at it, not sure what to do. I ponder over the decision until finally, I decide I will have to find out for sure before I tell the dragons. Otherwise, if it isn't him, then their relationship with him would be ruined for no reason. By the time I stumble into the healer's section, my head is pounding.

Anita darts toward me. "Kara, you look terrible." She grabs me by the arm to stop me from falling. "Come sit down over here." Gently, she leads me to a corner, bypassing the unconscious Rota and Prima, and sits me down on the chair.

I search every part of the room, and I can't seem to find my friends. "Where are Eir and Hildr?" I ask as the healer investigates my wounds.

"I've patched them up already. They are healing nicely. What happened to you?" A curly auburn strand of hair falls forward, hiding some of the concern in her green eyes. "I hope you weren't like this straight after the fight, or else you shouldn't have left."

"I... I... I don't know." Rubbing my head, I try to think. "I'm a little confused."

"Well, I'm not surprised. I hear that something weird happened up at that site."

"What did you hear?" My mind is filled with confusion as a piercing headache shoots through my frontal lobe.

"These two"—she indicates Rota and Prima—"have been touched by magic."

"How do you know?" I stare at them, but they are unmoving.

She gives me a strange look from the corner of her eye, and I get the feeling that she doesn't buy my innocence. "I've been healing long enough to see the signs of magic. I have been around much longer than you have." She joins me in staring at the two unconscious Valkyries. "The last time I saw something like this was back when dark elves attacked some Valkyries. They, too, were knocked unconscious. What I saw in Rota last night was the same but not to the same extent. The outcome manifesting today is much more intense than what she felt yesterday." She pauses, and I feel her eyes on me again. "I hear that it was you who touched Rota in the bathroom yesterday. And it was you who fought against them today, touching them and rendering them unconscious."

I rub my temples. "What is happening to me? How did I get magic? Valkyries don't have magic, do they? And if they do, what kind of magic do they have?" My questions come thick and fast, and I watch the healer's face, but it remains calm and collected while she processes each query.

"This is a strange world. Anything can happen in this realm. The nine realms have a mixture of gods, fairies, giants, and all sorts of odd creatures. I'm starting to think anything is possible." A drawer squeaks as she slides it open to retrieve a bandage, which she places beside me. "At times, all these things stretch my healing abilities to the limit, but it makes my job so interesting and rewarding when I manage to heal unusual wounds and illnesses."

"But I've never had magic before, and I haven't heard of other Valkyries having magic. How is this possible?"

Anita pulls back my sleeve, revealing my scar. "I think you know already." She rubs her thumb along the thick part of the scar then pushes my sleeve back down. "I think I remember you mentioning that a woman warned you about this mark earlier, and about the beast that caused it. Anybody who's been marked by this beast manifests magic eventually." She picks up a small flashlight and clicks it on before directing the light at one of my eyes then the other.

"But I don't know how to use magic." I glance at the two winged Valkyries that I had rendered unconscious. "I don't know how I could even hurt anybody with magic."

"Look back at the light." She directs the flashlight across my eyes a couple more times and places it down on the bench. "Sometimes, desperate situations require desperate measures and force us to bring out what is hidden—even without us intending it to manifest. From what I heard from Eir and Hildr, today's fight on the mountain wasn't fair. All the winged Valkyries stood against you, and you had no choice but to call forth whatever you could from within your body."

She pulls out some solution and cleans some of my smaller wounds. "If you ask me, I think they all deserved it. I also heard that your dragons came along to save the day." Smiling, she dabs some more ointment on my wounds. "I can't think of a better ending. Perhaps there is more to what you have been doing with these dragons. The bond is helping the wingless Valkyries to become more prominent. For centuries, winged Valkyries have been belittling the wingless Valkyries. It is about time someone strong enough stands up to them with the aid of a formidable partner that is strong enough to bring the winged Valkyries to their knees and realize how unjust they are. Then perhaps they will realize that the wingless Valkyries should be at the same level as them, not be looked down upon. Maybe then they can understand things can be better."

I flinch as she dabs at the wound on my torso that was created by the sword. "But why is this work allocated to me? I was only trying to get myself into Midgard to help serve Asgard and protect us from Ragnarök by reaping the souls of the warriors. I never intended any more than that. I don't understand how I managed to get caught up in this, causing the majority to gang up on my friends and me."

She stops dabbing ointment and begins to bandage my wounds. "That's what bullies do. And that's exactly how the winged Valkyries often treat the wingless Valkyries. They make things worse than what they originally were by trying to stop the person proving their value is more than what the bullies give them credit for. And in this case, because other, big factors are becoming involved, they may well be in for the shock of their lives. You make me excited just thinking about it."

Anita pulls the bandage tight and secures it with a clip. "As I said before, I am too old to be going into the fighting scene now, to try to reap souls for Valhalla, but I will certainly be here to mend your wounds and offer encouragement whenever I can. Come and use me as a counselor at any time." She smiles, and her face shines with kindness. "I will always be a friend you can talk to."

"Thank you, Anita. It's nice to hear that. To be honest, talking about it has lifted the cloud that was fogging my mind. Everything is a bit clearer now."

She finishes bandaging my wounds. "Now, I think you're fine. You should have these wounds healed in a few hours. You are not that knocked up, considering what you have just been through."

I huff a laugh. "You should see the other guy."

At first, she seems confused, and she gives me a sorrowful smile. "I think what you really need is rest. The lack of it is messing with your mind, and you need rest so your body can recuperate from using magic."

"Which reminds me." I frown. "Do you know where I can find Loki?"

She shakes her head. "He floats around a lot and is often hard to find. He even travels between the realms. Why?"

"No real reason. I just want to ask him a few things."

"Well, in the meantime, I have someone that I know can help you with training that magic," she says.

"You do?" I ask, shocked.

"Yes. He is rather strange, but I know he will help. He revels in magic's power and loves to share his ability and train people to use it. Here. I'll write the name down for you."

A piece of parchment crackles under her touch as she scribbles something on it and hands it to me. "Don't lose it."

After I take the note from Anita, I fold it then stuff it into the pocket of my pants. "Thank you. I'm going to get some rest."

I walk down the hallway after the promise of rest, and my curiosity gets the better of me. I pull the note out of my back pocket and study the name and the scribbled map to the address: Gilroma. *What an unusual name for an Asgardian.* I fold the parchment then place it back in my pocket and head out the door of the academy. I'm not going to rest before checking this out.

- CHAPTER THREE -

Shivers run up my spine as I follow an ominous tunnel. The wind whistles through the enclosed space, and goose bumps cover my skin. I pull the folded parchment from my pants pocket to check my progress. Dog-eared creases mark the corners, and it crackles its protest as I work in vain to return it to its original condition. Deep inside of me, I hope that I'm going in the wrong direction. This tunnel is giving me the creeps. My stomach feels queasy when the map confirms that I am going in the right direction. It takes all of my strength to remind myself why I am here, and curiosity finally wins. With my nerves barely intact, I push on, my feet stumbling on the jagged rocks. The tension from the eeriness stirs the magic in my arm.

Eventually, a small light glimmers, growing brighter as I slink closer. This tunnel is directly opposite the mountain where the fight was held earlier. Perhaps whoever was down here saw the fight. Rechecking the map, I confirm that this is the right direction. *Where has Anita sent me?* If I didn't trust Anita completely, I would be bolting out of here. The wind howls through the tunnel again. *This is so unnerving.*

Stopping, I straighten my shoulders and take a deep breath. I should've told someone I was coming here. But once again, my tendency to dive into something adventurous overtook me. I should have brought Hildr and Eir. But they're probably just as confused as I am over the magic. No, this is best done alone. I am the one that has the magic, not them, and I shouldn't put them at risk over something that is my problem.

I flick my fingers, trying to release the tension, and progress forward. The tunnel narrows, and the dull light flickering ahead is too dim to see clearly. I wish I'd brought a lamp.

After traveling several more feet, the tunnel encloses more, and I'm starting to doubt whether I'm in the right spot or have taken a wrong turn—except I didn't pass any turns. I pull out the scribbled map for what seems like the millionth time and take a look. Nope. It definitely says it is here.

For a moment, the light ahead glows brighter. I stop, trying to hear any sounds. "Hello?"

Silence is my answer. My arm starts to tingle, and the sensation pushes me forward despite my fear. The tingling spreads to my fingers, and I shake them out, but it continues. I begin to wonder if I'm in danger, because this is often what it does when I seem to be close to things of the dangerous kind.

I slowly press forward some more and call again, "Hello?"

Nothing. And despite my gut churning its disagreement, I continue to move forward. I'm determined to find out what to do with this magic. I am tired of it playing up regularly and twitching, like it needs my attention, and doing strange things when I don't expect it to. It acts as though I should automatically know what to do with it.

With each step forward, I try to avoid stumbling over the protruding rocks and reduce the amount of noise I am making. I cringe as a rock clatters after I kick it. My ears are on full alert as I try to listen for anything that may be ahead of me. I'm not sure if it is best that I arrive quietly, in case I run into something hostile, or if I should let Gilroma know I'm approaching.

Something rattles, and it sounds like a rock falling off other rocks. I pause and listen, but the sound has fallen silent. Perhaps it is an echo from the rock I knocked, or maybe it is the natural erosion of the mountain. This thought doesn't bring me comfort, but I continue anyway. More clattering sounds come from ahead.

"Hello? Is anybody there?"

Again, silence greets me. I'm getting tired of the unknown. I can't wait to reach the end of this tunnel. My body instinctively moves into defensive mode, hands ready, knees slightly bent with each step. I'm prepared to spring in any direction, eyes peeled for the slightest movement. It's drilled into us in battle training, causing it to become an automatic response anytime we feel insecure or threatened.

The tunnel turns a corner, and the top of the cave skims my head. I have to bend over slightly as I follow the light, which is brighter now.

Rounding another corner, I come upon a little room. Several candles are burning in different locations on the walls. All kinds of weird symbols and ornaments lie around the room, and a small pot has something simmering in the corner.

When I started this search for the reasoning behind the magic, I didn't know what to expect. I wasn't sure if I was going to find potions and herbs, but I don't see any sign of them lying within this room, and I wonder what kind of magic this person deals with and why they are so deep within this mountain.

I tuck my hair behind my ear, and the dark-brown locks fall over my shoulder. Dizziness overcomes me, and I press against the wall, holding my hand on my forehead. I wish I'd listened to Anita and had some rest instead of rushing into this.

Weird ornaments of different creatures line the room, their faces illuminated by several candles. My anxiety settles when I realize that no one is in this cave, ready to attack me, and I consciously work on catching my breath. I slide my back down the wall in the far corner and land on a flat rock.

My head is not clearing, and the prickling in my arm has intensified, reminding me of the sensation before I knocked a Valkyrie unconscious. I rest my head against the rock wall and take in the room. Nothing here makes me think of who might reside here. It's certainly no one I know. After I have taken everything in, I rest my elbows on my knees and hold my head between my hands as I gaze at the rocky floor. I have found myself in some strange situations over the last week or so, and I would never have thought my desire to help reap warriors for Valhalla and prove the worth of wingless Valkyries would turn my life this way.

After a while, my dizziness fades, and I study the room again. Over in the far corner, behind a pile of rocks, are the edges of a stack of books. I gather my strength and stand to have a look.

The top book has been left open, and it has images with intricate details of different weird things. After picking it up, I sit on the rocks and set the book on my lap. I mark the open page with my hand and close the book, unable to resist running my fingers over the design on the cover. A lot of work has gone into this weird embossed design, although it is strange. The spine is held together with straps of leather pinned to the front and back covers. On the top third, a strange-looking skull that looks as though it has been cut from a tree sends shivers up my arm as my fingers trail over the details.

I pull the front cover open and gaze at the title page. The words are in a language that I can't understand, but something about them pulls at something in my memory. The probing is unsuccessful in bringing it to the surface, so I run my fingers over the title page then slowly start to turn the thick parchment pages. The crackling of the pages sends excited anticipation running through my body. Unusual pictures cover each page, and strange writings hold my intrigue as I scan through the pages.

Something in the corner of a page catches my eye. It almost looks like an underlined eye with slashes through it. As I stare at it, it dawns on me that this image is a symbol of the dark elves. It means "I am one with the darkness."

My face loses feeling, and my mind races. I can't help wondering if I'm in danger right now. Surely not. Anita wouldn't have sent me somewhere that would put me in danger. She offered to heal my wounds and support me with my cause. The more I think about it, the harder I find it to believe that she would send me somewhere dangerous on purpose.

I focus my thoughts and study the book some more. The language in this book must belong to the dark elves. They hold magic, but I have only heard of evil dark elves—ones who want to destroy the Valkyries or anybody in Asgard. *Is the occupier of this cave a dark elf wanting to destroy Asgard and its occupants? Or is it a hobby of theirs to collect items belonging to the dark elves and learn their language? Maybe they are obsessed with their magic.*

Resting my head against the rock wall for a while, I ponder everything that has happened. It has been a very eventful day, and perhaps I am reading too much into this. Or maybe I'm not, and I should escape this cave before it is too late. This might not be the best place for me to be.

Images run through my head of what Odin and Mistress Sigrun would do if they found out where I am. Despite their certain disapproval, I can't squash my burning curiosity, and I flick through a few more pages before setting the book aside. I reach for another book, curious to see what lies within its pages. Each page I turn is filled with the language of the dark elves. Some of the images are disturbing, with someone's flesh melting away from the bone. A sick feeling rises in my stomach, and I close the book and stack it neatly in the corner with the others.

The itch to leave grows strong. Magic or no magic, I don't think this is a place for me. I rise and make my way toward the door, observing the strange figurines as I pass. Perhaps I should research these in the Valkyrie library. As I reach the entrance of the room, a noise sounds around the corner. Pausing, I listen, and it sounds again. This time, I am sure I hear footsteps crunching the rocks on the floor of the cave. I back into the room and press my back against the stone wall on the same side as the door. There is no way out. Whatever is coming, I have no choice but to deal with it.

- CHAPTER FOUR -

My nails scratch the wall as my fingers hunt for security by trying to dig into its surface. With each approaching footstep, my shallow breaths rasp, and I steer my focus to calm them, keeping them deep and quiet, but I struggle, and my heartbeat quickens. I'm trapped in this cave, forced to wait for whatever is around the corner. Some more rocks clatter. I don't know if it is a dark elf or something else. Whoever it is, they are almost here. I push even farther back against the cold stones, and the footfalls pause just around the corner.

"I can smell you, my dear. I can smell your fear." The voice is raspy and tainted with intrigue.

His words don't make me feel better.

"Oh, stop it! You just got worse. It was meant to calm you, my dear." Amusement mixes with curiosity in his voice. "I'm coming in, so don't attack. I'm not going to hurt you."

True to his word, he enters the room, and I gasp. He is a dark elf but nothing like I expected. The dark elves that I have seen in pictures often have long, luscious hair that falls past their shoulders, and their physique is usually thin. This dark elf is stockier, his head bald and his cheeks scarred. His eyes are sunken, and deep gashes line his cheeks in vertical stripes. I stare at the tattoos that run along his cheekbones from his eyes to his mouth like jagged tear streaks pointing to his jaw, which is lined with warrior tattoos. A symbol resembling the head of a trident with spiky prongs decorates his forehead, with a hollow directly over his "third eye."

As impressive and intimidating as these tattoos are, they can't hold my attention like his glowing yellow eyes. They narrow, and he enters slowly, his eyes never straying from mine. Despite his promise to not harm me, each step he takes doesn't allay my fear. Something about the glowing yellow eyes and warrior tattoos makes me feel uncomfortable. A long crimson gown flaps quietly with each movement and covers his long, flowing charcoal pants and matching long-sleeved top, which is open to the waist, showing off his muscular chest and two dangling silver chains. He tugs at the two black hoop earrings hanging from his pointy left ear.

"Gilroma?"

"In the flesh." He gives a mocking bow, his eyes never leaving me.

I steel my courage and take a deep breath. "You know, staring at me like that is not making me feel any more relaxed." My voice sounds calmer than I feel, showing my expertise in bluffing my confidence.

His eyes soften at the edges, and he waves a hand at me. "Oh, relax! I'm not going to hurt you." This time he sounds more upbeat and sincere and, somehow, less creepy.

Refusing to let my stare drop, I make sure to read all of his body language to see if he is telling the truth. Something is familiar about him, but I don't know what. Surely I would remember someone with glowing yellow eyes. "Have I seen you before?" I ask.

"I doubt it," the dark elf says. "I tend to keep a low profile. The likes of me are not necessarily welcome in Asgard, which is why I have adopted such a secluded and secure place to reside in." He lifts his palms, indicating the room. "It keeps me safe from the menacing Valkyries and gods who think they know better."

"I can't imagine why you're not welcome." Sarcasm oozes from my voice.

His hairless eyebrows lift with intrigue as he enters the room farther, leaving the entry open and giving me the option of escape. "Although I enjoy a visit from a friendly face, there must be a reason why you have come here."

I lift my chin slightly. "I was told this is where I could find some answers."

He clasps his hands behind his back and stands in the middle of the room, blocking my view of the books. "About what?"

Even though I am here to learn, my tongue remains idle, and my eyes betray me, darting to where I know the books lie behind him.

"It's all right, my dear. I will not harm you. I can sense the question raging within your mind. In fact, I think I can answer it for you without you having to voice it." He lifts his large nose and sniffs deeply. "I can smell the magic on you."

I frown. "What? How can you smell it on me? What kind of nose do you have?"

"They should teach you more in Valkyrie school. You Valkyries tend to be so focused on just one thing that you forget that there is more to life than reaping souls for Valhalla." He flicks his cape over his shoulder, revealing more of his clothes.

"Well, they don't. You mustn't be worth much to the Valkyries, or else they would teach us about you." The words come out harsher than I meant. I don't know why I'm being so snarky. He hasn't made any indication that he wants to hurt me. Perhaps it is a replacement for my fear.

The dark elf sits in the far corner of the room, his eyes never leaving me, then holds his hands out toward my left side. "Why don't you step forward and show me that hand of yours?"

Stunned, I ask, "How do you know it is that hand?"

"I have a way of sensing things."

Eyeing him suspiciously, I decide to step forward and hold out my hand. He clasps my wrist and flips it over to turn the palm face up then uses his other hand to trace a circle in the center. A tingling feeling surges up my arm, bounces within the confines of my skull, and shoots back down my arm and into my hand. My body lurches slightly backward as white light fires out of my palm and into the air, narrowly missing the dark elf's face when he pulls to the side just in time.

I gawk at my palm in shock. "It's never done that before."

"And it shouldn't. You must get control over this magic. You could harm yourself and many others you care about if you don't learn how to use it properly. Whoever sent you here is right to do so. They had your best interests in mind." His wide eyes don't leave me.

"What?" I ask. "Why are you looking at me like that?"

His hairless eyebrows rise. "I have a good idea of who might've sent you. You don't need to tell me the name. I know of a wingless Valkyrie within your academy who is fond of anyone pushing the boundaries against the winged Valkyries and their rules."

I raise an eyebrow right back at him. "And who do you think that might be?"

"Someone I have helped with addressing magic abilities before. Your healer is quite resourceful. Use her wisely. She makes a great ally."

"I'll keep that in mind. Although I'm already starting to get that impression." I have no reason to deny what this dark elf already knows.

"Good. Let's have a look and see what you can do."

I observe my hand. A swelling mark in the shape of a whirl lies in the middle of my palm. "Did you do that?"

The dark elf almost looks hurt. "I merely traced a mark so your magic has a portal to come out. You've been marked before." His hand slides up my arm, and I flinch. He stops and looks at me. "It's okay. I won't hurt you."

I grit my teeth, and eventually, I nod.

His hand travels farther up my arm, revealing my scar. "This is where you've been marked before. I have merely made a spot on your palm so your existing magic has a place to escape more directly rather than only through emotion. Once you have learned to use this wisely, we shall look at other avenues."

I flip my palm over and rub my thumb slowly over the new mark. "Why didn't I see the white light come out before when I used my magic?"

"Because it didn't have a clear release. There were small barriers in play that caused some of the magic to bounce back within you."

"Then wouldn't I have knocked myself unconscious?"

"No, because it is already a part of you, and you are filled with this magic. What you hit your enemies with was only a diluted solution of your pure magic. So you need to control this. Control the strength that you allow to exit your body, and also what you can do with it and how you direct it."

I gulp. "Do you mean I could have done worse to Rota and Prima? I didn't mean to harm them any more than to get them to leave me alone. I didn't want to hurt them that much."

He nods. "I know. You're lucky that you've been directed here."

"Do you know this creature that marked me?"

"Yes." He studies me again. "Why?"

"Why would it mark me?"

"The creature only marks someone they think is worthy."

"But I was fighting the creature. It was going to steal one of the emperor dragon's eggs. Why would it see me as someone to mark? I thought it was attacking me, not marking me."

A strange smirk that makes me uncomfortable crosses the dark elf's face, but I ignore it. "Clearly, the creature saw something of value in you, something that not even you see, and it decided that you were worth marking."

I struggle to understand this, and I frown.

Ignoring me, he continues as though nothing is unusual. "I want to concentrate on the magic welling in your arm. Now that you have this mark in your hand, I want you to concentrate on the magic in your arm and that tingling sensation you're feeling." He runs a finger up and down my arm. The tingling feeling ignites farther to the top of my shoulder. "I want you to gather it and hang on to it."

I focus on the sensation, imagining walls enclosing around it, feeling the power swell.

"How are you doing with that?" he asks.

"I think I'm gathering it, but I'm not sure. I've never done this before."

"Okay. After you think you've gathered it into a concentrated ball and feel that the power is ready to burst through the edges, concentrate on that far wall. Then aim your palm at the wall before shooting your magic out of your palm and onto that spot."

I squint at the spot on the wall, picturing it in my head, and follow his instructions precisely, shooting a bolt of white light out of my hands and into the wall. A large chunk of the wall crumbles and falls to the hard floor.

"Oh, Vanir!" My mouth drops open.

- CHAPTER FIVE -

By the time I leave the cave, I'm elated with power and a dangerous sense of invincibility. I have learned to control a small amount of my magic with the dark elf's help, and I can't wait to share my experience with Hildr, Eir, and Elan. So much has happened that it almost seems as though I have left them behind without meaning to. I stumble along the rocky tunnel as I rush to see them, remembering that my curiosity was so piqued that I didn't even call in on them after they were discharged from the healing ward.

Finally, I stumble out of the long, dingy tunnel into the sunlight, welcoming the warmth that hits me fully in the chest and fills me with more cheer. I feel across my torso where the sunlight hits my bare skin. The wounds I had before I ran into the elf have disappeared, not only aided by my Valkyrie blood but also accelerated by Gilroma's magic. Turning my face toward the sun, I close my eyes and smile. I can feel the magic, no longer an object of fear, surging through me.

Heading toward my room in the Valkyrie Academy, I pass several winged Valkyries who stare at me with disdain as I walk down the corridors. I lift my chin. It's not my fault that they cheated, causing me to unleash my magic before the dragons decided to join in and help us.

As one of them stares at me, I return her gaze. "What's wrong? Didn't the dragons beat you up enough the first time? Would you like me to bring them around so you can receive a second beating?"

Her mouth drops open, and I smile, thinking I must be succeeding in annoying them and putting a stop to how they treat us. I smirk. *Good. It's about time.* I've come a long way since Rota, Prima, and Mist tried to give me a swirly the other day.

My shoes clop as I charge into our bedroom, and I spot Hildr and Eir sitting on their beds with bandages covering different parts of their bodies. For a moment, I am taken aback and halt at the door, staring at them. The bandages give the impression that they were hurt worse than I thought. "Are you guys healing okay?"

Hildr's pale, freckly face flushes as she notices that I am staring at the bandages. She glances down then looks back up with a guilty look on her face. "Oh, yeah. We're healing just

49

fine. We just haven't taken them off yet." She unwraps a bandage and shows me the spot underneath. It has healed perfectly.

"Then why are you still in our room?" I ask.

Eir's long, wavy locks of light-brown hair fall over her face as she feels along her bandages, checking for any residual wounds on her skin. "Because we are physically tired and weary of them making jeering comments as we walk down in the corridor." Her face screws up in disappointment. "You know, because we were beaten in battle—especially me."

"You shouldn't be bummed at all. Both you and Hildr did well." I place a hand on her shoulder.

"No, you nailed it." Hildr's green eyes fill with shame as she shakes her head and looks down at her blankets.

It kills me to see them this way. There is no trace of Hildr's fighting spirit. I'm determined to lift their dispositions. "Only with help from you guys, and with the dragons. If it weren't for a united effort, I wouldn't have nailed it."

Hildr scoffs. "It has nothing to do with you being a magic holder as well."

I twist to look at her directly, dumbfounded.

"Yeah, we have heard about that," Eir says sadly. "Everyone is telling us about how you used magic to wipe out Rota and Prima."

Holding my palm up, I gaze down at the new whirl drawn on it. "You're kind of right. Something weird is going on with my hand — some sort of magic. But I still wouldn't have nailed it without help from you guys and the dragons." I pull my gaze from my palm and take turns looking at them. "You should be proud of that. You helped heaps. It was only three of us against all of them, not a fair fight at all."

My heart drops when I noticed that they still don't believe me. I try to think of anything that will cheer them up. "One thing you two did miss out on was how the dragons helped. Naga was especially entertaining. He flew around the circle of the winged Valkyries and head-butted each one out of their positions." I chuckle. "If only you could have seen them flying sideways. It made it easier to defend against our true challengers."

The horn rings out across the land, and my heart skips a beat. I can't believe it. It is the horn for Midgard, and we were promised a clean entry if we defeated the winged Valkyries.

I turn to the other two expectantly. "Who's coming?"

They shake their heads in unison.

"We don't get to come," Eir says.

"Yes, we do." I place my hands on my hips. "We defeated them even though it was an unfair fight."

"No, *you* defeated them." Hildr's freckled face sets with disappointment, and I struggle with this image. It is a strange sight when her spiky red hair is usually matched with determination. "You get to go. We'll go visit our dragons, I guess."

They stand to leave, and my heart caves with sadness for them. "One day, we will get you there. You deserve to go just as much as me and any winged Valkyries."

"We'll see. At least we have our dragons to go to." Hildr straps on her sword sheath, probably more out of habit than anything, before leaving with Eir.

After replacing my damaged leather clothes with new ones, I race to my bed and grab my dragon-scale cloak, my bow and quiver, and my sword and throw them over my back. I attach my sling to my back pants pocket, and I charge down the hall while throwing my scale cape on. This time, the hallway is empty of all the winged Valkyries, leaving me to run down the corridor without their torments and glares.

I bolt straight for the place where Elan usually sunbathes. It seems to be her favorite spot. I don't see her, but knowing she could be invisible, I call, "Elan!"

It doesn't take long until her scales start to shift into view. *What is it?* Her voice sounds in my head.

"We need to get to Heimdall's post right away."

Why?

"We need to ride Bifrost to get to Midgard and help reap warrior souls for Valhalla." I strap on the saddle then climb up and throw my leg over her back, hooking my feet into the stirrups. "I want to make the most of my newfound access."

She pushes off the ground and climbs into the air, heading straight for Heimdall's post. For only a moment, the wind thrums noisily against my ear, and I pull my hood over my head, restricting its effect. Even though I shouldn't be surprised, I am amazed at how little time flying takes compared to my usual task of climbing up the cliff face and running across the plains. It seems like only seconds before the ride ends and Elan is landing in front of Asgard's sentinel.

I remain on Elan's back as Heimdall's hands rest on the hilt of his sword, which balances point first on the ground. His dark-brown eyes stare at me from under his horned helmet, then he looks at Elan and back at me. "Young Valkyrie. What is the meaning of this?"

"Heimdall. I defeated the winged Valkyries in competition, and Mistress Sigrun agreed that if I did so, I would be able to go to Midgard to help with the battle and to reap the souls of Valhalla."

Confusion flicks across his face.

"I intend to start today and to make sure she honors this agreement."

Heimdall's body freezes briefly as he ponders this information. His eyes take on a darker shade as he stares at me then back at my dragon. The moments that pass seem like an eternity. "I do not believe that you are telling me another fib, young Valkyrie. I find it hard to believe that you are so dumb as to do this if you didn't have the right of passage. I will grant you the right this time. If I hear differently, there will be consequences to pay."

"I understand," I say. "Thank you, Heimdall. You are making the right decision."

The gatekeeper opens the entrance to Bifrost, and Elan struggles to squeeze through the portal. Instantly, we are sucked down a massive slide, and after a few seconds, we land hard on Midgard's strangely green surface lined with trees that obscure any view to the battlefield. I scan the surface and take a deep breath before letting out a contented sigh. The air has a fresh, light smell to it. "This planet is vastly different from Asgard and utterly beautiful."

Oh, I like it! Elan's eyes are wide as she scans the horizon.

When I notice that she is visible, I chuckle. "I think you might scare the residents, Elan."

Then maybe I should disappear. She turns invisible.

"Yes, I think that's the best option for now. Let's find the battlefield."

Elan's body moves to face the bushes. *What kind of stuff is that?* She huffs, and before I can stop her, fire shoots out of her mouth, setting the bush on fire.

"Elan!" I cry, sliding off her back, then I remove my scaled cloak and hit the flames with it.

Whoops! That was very flammable.

"Yes, Midgard is extremely flammable." I hit the bushes a few more times, managing to put out the last of the flames. "You can't do that. It is such a beautiful place."

I didn't mean to wreck it.

"I know." Watching the spots where the fire used to be, I slide the cloak back on. "It's out now." I climb onto her back and spread the cloak out around me. Noticing how it covers the saddle and some of the straps, I smile, proud of my handiwork. The scale cape completely covers everything vital. "Let's go and fight."

You betcha! Elan says.

I kick my heels lightly against her flank, and she pushes off into the air.

- CHAPTER SIX -

As Elan flies into the air in her invisible form,

I pull the hood of my cape over my head and keep my ears tuned, listening for the cries of war. Eventually, I hear them not too far away from where we landed in Midgard. We follow the screams to find a primal scene of people fighting with swords and archers lining the outskirts, shooting people with arrows.

Valkyries and angels of death are flying above the fighting field and landing in different places. There are many warriors to choose from, but each time a Valkyrie and an angel of death land next to the same soldier, a fight erupts.

A Valkyrie lands next to a soldier she wants and begins to reap his soul, but she is interrupted by an angel of death, and they clash swords over the warrior, who is approaching his final breaths. Pain shoots in my stomach. This warrior's pain can be taken from him in an instant, except he has to wait for the battle for his soul to be finalized, if he can hold out that long. It is a scene that is being replayed many times over the field, sometimes with the angel of death being the first to arrive at the soldier's side.

I see no sign of Rota, Prima, or Mist. A small twinge of guilt pulls at my heart when I realize that Rota and Prima are probably still in the healing ward, recovering from my magic.

A puff of steam erupts in front of me. *This is barbaric,* Elan says. *And I thought dragons were terrible. Do you really want to be part of this?*

"Being barbaric is not what I have in mind. My goal is to prove wingless Valkyries are just as valuable to the cause of saving us from Ragnarök."

There must be a better way to do it.

I shake my head then realize that she probably isn't looking at me. "No. This is all Valkyries are bred for—to reap the souls of the brave warriors so they can fight and defend Asgard in the final battle."

Okay. If that's what you need to do, then let's do it.

Elan flies in, grabs an angel of death by the shoulders, and flings him aside. His body pivots, and his eyes widen as he is tossed, back first, toward a tree.

"What are you doing?" I watch the angel as he spreads his wings to soften the blow and searches for the cause of his sudden change of direction.

I'm helping. She swoops down, aiming straight for the next angel of death in line, and picks him up by the shoulders and flings him beside the last one.

It surprises me that they don't see me in the saddle before being snatched from their duty. The last one looked directly at me but still didn't flinch when my body dived at him. He continued as if I didn't exist.

After flinging that angel of death aside, Elan flaps her mighty wings, and we lift into the sky and circle the battlefield before aiming for another angel.

Can't I just breathe fire over them? That would be fun.

"No, don't do that. I don't want to kill the angels of death. I only want them to get away from the souls that we are trying to reap."

You take all the fun out of it, Elan says with lighthearted disappointment.

"I guess. If that's what you call fun."

My stomach lurches as she dives to the next angel of death, and he looks up, a puzzled expression on his face.

As we near him, it occurs to me that I know this one. "Elan! Stop!"

She is only seconds away from gabbing him by his shoulders. His face remains turned up with a strange expression, but he doesn't recognize me, even though I am sure it is him. Elan swoops up at the last second, narrowly avoiding his shoulders.

A Valkyrie darts at him with a sword in her hand, and I call, "Harut! Look out!"

The puzzled look remains on his face as he searches around him and spots the Valkyrie a few feet away. She swings at him with her sword, and he retrieves his in time to block the blow. The sound of clanging metal echoes across the valley.

"Can you break that up, please, Elan?" The tingling surges in my left palm. I can feel the magic stirring inside me.

What? That is a strange request.

"I want to get closer to stop this fight. This angel of death has done a favor for me before, and I would like to return it."

Okay. She circles around and lands on a patch where no one is fighting, not far from Harut. *Since when have you known an angel of death?*

"It's a long story. I'll tell you later." I swing my leg over her back and slide down. My feet hit the ground with a soft thud, and the grass crunches under my boots as I head toward him. I clench fists as I watch the Valkyrie swinging at him with full force. He stops the blow in time and fights back. His fighting skills are impressive, but I still don't like seeing him put in danger. I know from experience that these Valkyries will fight to the death.

My left arm is burning with magic, and I'm dying to throw some magic at the Valkyrie. Thanks to the dark elf, I have perfected my aim. I tug at the hood of my cloak, securing its protection of my head and neck. A surge of confidence rises with each rub of the cloak against my legs. "Stop!" I call.

The battle is too intense at this point, and neither of them stops their attack. I rush forward, darting between them and dodging the blade of the sword. Harut's sword swipes along the dragon scales of my coat. "Stop!" I call again.

The Valkyrie's retaliation swings toward me, and her blade stops in midair.

Her eyes narrow when they focus on me. "Step away, wingless. You shouldn't be here."

"You know I have permission to be here." I remain between them and cross my arms. "That was the agreement if I beat Rota, Prima, and Mist. Not only did we beat them, but we also proved that we can still succeed with all of you winged Valkyries going against us in an unfair fight."

When I approach her, she backs away with her sword held high. "Don't you dare touch me with those hands." She glares at them with a look of disgust.

"What's the matter? Are you afraid that you'll end up like Prima or Rota?" I tilt my head to the side.

"I don't know how you came across such power, but you shouldn't have it. Your side wasn't fair either. You brought magic to the ring, like some witch or dark elf."

"So you're afraid of a wingless Valkyrie with a little bit of power. Now there's a change." I have no desire to use my magic on her, especially if she leaves Harut or me alone, but a small part of me is happy to see her cringe after how they have treated the wingless Valkyries in general.

"You still shouldn't be here," she snaps before pushing into the air and flying in retreat.

Behind me, Harut looks confused as he observes me with a raised eyebrow and his sword still hanging by his side. When I remove the hood from my head, letting it fall to my shoulders, he smiles, his pale cheeks puffing out, and his dark eyes dance with amusement. "It's nice to see a friendly face in this battle," he says while tucking his black wings closer to his back.

Elan is visible behind him, and her upper lip screws up into what looks like a snarl, except her eyes don't hold viciousness. She looks at me and says, *There's a rotten smell coming from that direction,* then turns invisible again.

I chuckle. That was such an odd thing to do.

Harut's black eyes search my body as he observes me and my cloak. Heat rises to my cheeks. "What are you wearing?"

Welcoming a distraction, I look at the sleeves of my cloak. "This is just something I've made."

"It's an odd choice, but I like it."

I laugh nervously. It would seem like an odd choice to him because he hasn't seen Elan. "I've made friends with a dragon, and I made a cape from their scales. It acts as a shield, except it is lighter in weight, and it protects more of my body."

"What a brilliant idea." He circles me, taking in the details, then stops in front of me. "How did you get here?"

"On the back of my dragon."

His face drops. "There's a dragon here?"

I nod. "Yes."

He searches the field and the sky. "Where?"

"She's invisible."

"Invisible? She has that ability?"

"Yes. She was staring at you before."

His face somehow turns paler. "Before when?"

"You were looking up into the sky, and we were coming straight at you, just before the Valkyrie attacked you.

His forehead crinkles into a frown. "I didn't see you, but I did see some strange strap things floating through the sky."

I point behind him, and he turns. "Like those straps?"

"Yes. It was like those but without the saddle." His voice is hesitant, as though he thinks he is seeing things.

I chuckle, as the saddle sitting in midair does look strange. "Elan, can you show yourself?"

For a moment, Elan's golden scales shimmer in the sun, and she glowers at Harut before disappearing again. I shake my head and smile. Elan is doing her intimidating introduction she loves so much.

"Holy Freyja! She's one vicious-looking dragon." He backs away from her and looks at me. "I knew you were different."

Frowning, I ask, "You mean because I don't have wings?"

He shakes his head. "Well, there's that, but no. You just had something different about you. I never would've guessed it would be because you befriended a dragon." His eyes stray for a moment as he gazes over the battlefield. "And I'm guessing you're here to prove that you are worthy again." He looks at me again with a questioning look on his face.

"You got it!"

Indicating the soldier lying on the ground, the one he had been fighting over, he says, "Be my guest."

"Really?"

He nods.

"But won't it upset your leader or something?"

He smirks. "Don't worry about that. I'll deal with them." He nods again to the soldier, who groans loudly as though on cue. "Please, be my guest. Let's see if this magic that Valkyrie was talking about helps you reap souls."

- CHAPTER SEVEN -

With shaking hands, I approach the moaning soldier. A large gash lines his torso, exposing his intestines. There is no hope for him on Midgard, and he needs to be released from his pain.

"I can sense an honorable side to him." Staring at him, I take in all of his features. He has the harsh face of a warrior in his thirties, but there is something different, possibly softer in the lines around his eyes.

"Yes, that is correct. The angels of death target the more honorable and less ruthless souls to reap because that is what Freyja wants for Folkvangr."

I gaze over my shoulder at him. "From what they teach us at Valkyrie Academy, the Valkyries go for the savage, fearless warriors."

"Yes, that is right. You are a bloodthirsty lot."

"Then why do Valkyries and angels of death fight over warriors?"

The soldier moans again, and I return my gaze to him.

"Because if they are strong, then the Valkyries will also want that soul. Your kind is also a greedy lot."

I frown. After hearing that, I would have to agree with him. I focus and remind myself that I'm here to prove the other wingless Valkyries' and my worth. I'm not going to let an opportunity go to waste. Placing a shaking hand on one of his, I brush the hair off his forehead before resting my left palm there.

Blood is trickling down his face, and his pale-blue eyes stare up at me. The pain on his face screams so loudly that I almost feel it in my body. I concentrate hard on the magic tingling in my left arm as it moves toward my hand.

Leaning close to his ear, I whisper to him, "I release you from your pain on Earth and send you to Valhalla to serve amongst the bravest of warriors."

I wait—and I wait some more. Nothing happens. The soldier groans, and a deep twist of guilt knots through my stomach. I haven't relieved him of his pain. *How can this be?* I can't relieve him, even with magic and the right to join the Valkyries on the battlefield. But I thought that my magic could send him to Valhalla, or at least prove my right to be here with the winged Valkyries. I release a small amount of magic into him, giving it another go. He cries in pain, and I stop instantly, staring at my hands. I'm not trying to kill him—I'm trying to reap him and relieve his pain. I'm disheartened deep to my core—not only for me but also for him.

Harut squats next to me, and he places a hand on my shoulder. A strange kind of cold warmth flows through my body. "There must be more to it than what they are telling you."

"Or what they're not telling me," I say.

"Wingless!"

The familiar voice screeches across the distance, and I exhale deeply. That voice always brings trouble for me. Slowly, I turn my eyes up to see Mistress Sigrun stomping my way, her tan leather jacket flapping against her waist.

"What are you doing?"

I push up to stand, and Harut stands next to me.

Squaring my shoulders, I say, "I am entitled to be here. I won the right, remember?" I narrow my eyes as she crosses her arms and holds her chin high. "You agreed in front of all of the academy. Are you planning on breaking that agreement?"

She raises her chin some more, her blue eyes sharp. "You didn't win properly. You had help."

"And so did Rota, Prima, and Mist. They were supposed to be the only ones fighting. Instead, all of you winged Valkyries stood against us. It was only once the dragons realized that you weren't playing fair and outnumbered us that they intervened. Otherwise, it would have been our lives."

"And that would have been three lives not missed," the mistress says. She leans to the side, placing all of her weight on one hip, and her royal-blue leather pants squeak from the movement.

"Did you really just say that?" Harut moves in front of me, blocking the mistress.

"Stay out of it, angel of death." She turns to the Valkyrie Harut fought earlier. "Reap him." She indicates the soldier still moaning on the ground.

Harut blocks her path to the soldier. "No. You may not reap him. He's mine."

"Out of the way, angel of death," Mistress Sigrun demands then unsheathes her sword and holds it menacingly in front of Harut.

I step in front of the mistress and hold up my left palm. The circle on it glows. "Step back, Mistress. This is Harut's soul. It is his right. He was only giving it to me."

"If he has given it to you, then he has given it to all the Valkyries. Step out of the way, wingless." She glares at me.

I raise my left palm more, and she backs away. "What? Are you going to use magic on me now?"

A corner of my mouth lifts. "If I have to." I wave my palm. "The Valkyries don't want this soul, anyway. He is gentler than the normal soul that you need for Valhalla. He is more of a friend and a lover. Someone with compassion. Not a typical Valkyrie requirement for a soldier of Valhalla."

The mistress stares at my palm then at the soldier before staring at my palm again. She crosses her arms and puts her weight on one leg. "Then you can have the dregs, angel of death."

Harut squats and reaps the soldier. A tinge of jealousy sweeps over me as I watch the warrior's face turn peaceful.

The mistress stares at my cape with an upturned nose. "How did you get here, wingless? It would take flying power to get here as quickly as you did."

"I came here on my dragon."

"Of course you did. Go home, wingless," she snaps then flies away, her beautiful white wings shining in the sun.

My gaze falls to the dead soldier, and I'm frustrated that I still can't reap souls—after everything I've done to get here.

Harut's concerned black eyes watch me. It's strange that one who is considered my enemy is the only friendly one here, except Elan. "Are you all right?" he asks.

I nod, even though my heart is tearing apart over another failure.

"Come." He reaches for my hand, and a strange tingling sensation shoots up my right arm, making it feel numb. It's a different sensation from what happens in the left one. This sensation rushes from my arm and through my torso, and I can feel the blood rushing to my ears.

I pull my hood over my head, and I catch a glimpse of his eyes as he looks at the intricate detail of my cape.

"You've made an interesting cape. It looks even more beautiful in the sun. I don't know how I didn't see it earlier if you were flying straight at me."

"You have me baffled. Only Elan, my dragon, can turn invisible."

The battle continues to rage around us, and I find my interest has wavered for the moment.

"Shouldn't you be reaping more souls?" I ask.

He surveys the field. "The battle is almost finished. There aren't too many souls left to reap. The other angels of death can take care of this."

We stroll toward the saddle. It's sitting strangely off to the side of the battlefield, on the invisible Elan's back. When we reach Elan, she turns visible for a moment. I clasp onto the saddle and climb up then stick my feet into the stirrups and spread my cloak over the sides, covering the saddle. Elan disappears underneath me, and I peer at Harut through the corner of my eye.

"So what do you think?"

He shakes his head. "I now know why I couldn't see you."

- CHAPTER EIGHT -

Frowning, I observe Harut from the corner of my eye. "What do you mean?"

He opens his arms wide. "You're invisible."

I turn to face him fully. "What?"

He chuckles. "Well, everywhere your cloak covers is invisible. I can see your face, though, now that you're looking at me."

"Are you serious?" Gazing down, I can't see Elan, but I can see myself. "Elan, can you turn visible, please?"

Elan's golden scales glitter in the sun. "Can you see me now?" I ask Harut.

"Now, I can see you. Yes." He nods. "Why don't you try it again?"

"Elan, can you turn invisible?" I ask. The golden glow disappears from below me, and the green grass of Midgard replaces her scales.

"Yup, you're definitely invisible again," Harut states before I can ask him.

"Huh. Imagine that. Can you please turn visible again?"

Elan's glow appears in front of me again, and I climb down from her back. I stroke her side and rest my hand on her shoulder, making sure my cloak touches her scales. "Elan, can you please turn invisible again?" Her scales disappear in front of my eyes, and I ask Harut, "What about now? Can you see me?"

"No. I can't see you. I can see your face when you look at me, but if you pull your hood over your face, I can't see you at all."

"Imagine that. I've made something more important than I thought." I pull my hand away from Elan, so the scales of my cloak are not touching her. "What about now?"

"Yup. You're visible again."

I walk around to Elan's snout. "Did you know about this, Elan?"

She shakes her head. *I see our scales regularly on the ground in the wastelands, but I never thought to see if they would turn invisible when our invisible bodies were touching them.* She huffs, and a puff of smoke shoots out of her nostrils. *Can I ask you a favor?*

"Of course."

Can you ask your friend to stand downwind? He stinks.

I chortle and feel the blood rush to my cheeks over the thought of passing this embarrassing information over to him. "What do you mean?"

He stinks of death.

I gaze at Harut with confusion. *How can someone who looks so handsome smell disgusting?* I noticed an odor of rotting flesh at different stages on the battlefields, but I didn't connect it to him or the other angels of death.

"You look as though you're talking to your dragon," he says.

I forgot to tell him. It completely slipped my mind. "Yes. Sorry. I assumed that she was sharing the conversation with you too. Elan speaks in my head." I frown at her. She shared the conversations she held with me in front of Hildr and Eir in their heads, yet now that she wants to say something embarrassing, she only tells me and asks me to pass the message on.

Harut moves cautiously closer to Elan. "She does? What is she saying?"

"I don't really think you want to know," I say, trying to give him a reassuring smile, but I know I've failed.

"Sure I do." He moves closer. "I've never spoken to a dragon before. I had no idea they could speak."

"Um… well." I search my mind desperately for how to say this politely. I've only spent a small amount of time with Harut, and he has treated me well on the battlefields. Since I've grown quite fond of him, the last thing I want to do is upset him. "Um."

Elan shakes her head. *I said that you smell, angel of death. And I need you to move downwind.* Elan's voice booms through my head, and the breath catches in my throat when I look at Harut. She must have shared this conversation with him.

Harut's gaze drops to the ground, and his cheeks redden. "Oh. Now I understand why you didn't want to tell me." His shoulders slump. "Unfortunately, that's an occupational hazard. I had forgotten about it because we never communicate with other species." He turns to leave. "I'm sorry."

Holding out a hand to stop him, I say, "I don't mind. Well, um, I do mind the smell, but I'm not going to avoid you because of it." My tongue trips over the words. "Just because my friends have something wrong with them doesn't mean I'm going to turn them away. Although I would be happier if you stayed downwind from me if you smell like corpses that have been rotting for several days."

His face turns red, and he looks as though he's about to turn away again.

"I'm sorry. That came out completely wrong."

"No. That's okay. I know it's the truth. It's just embarrassing." Gradually, he moves downwind, his eyes not meeting mine.

Silence fills the air as we fidget awkwardly, and I try to think of a way to change the topic. I feel so bad, and I glare at Elan.

After a while, Harut breaks the silence. "How did you manage to get magic? The other Valkyries have talents in fighting and reaping souls, but none of them seem to have magic." He indicates the Valkyries aggressively finishing their fight. "Do all wingless Valkyries have magic?"

"No. I'm different. A beast marked me, and I've only just discovered it. It's a long story. Let's sit and talk about it."

We sit close to Elan and rest our backs against a tree.

"Actually, before we start, did I see you in the portal of Bifrost not so long ago?" I ask. "It was so strange. Heimdall was refusing to let me go to Midgard, and as he stood in my way, your image appeared in the middle of the portal and seemed to hover there for a few moments."

"Yes. That was me. I thought you saw me. I came looking for you. I was hoping that you would turn up to the next battle on Midgard, but you didn't come. So I tried to come to Asgard without permission." He chuckles. "You should be grateful for your gatekeeper. He is one tough cookie to get past." He holds up a finger and smirks. "But I did manage to spot you through the portal, and I could see you were having trouble getting past him too."

My cheeks heat when I think of him going all the way to Asgard's portal to see me. "Oh. That's sweet."

His eyes travel over my face, and the warmth in my cheeks intensifies. I don't know what's wrong with me. He smiles then stands, and the grass crunches under his feet as he moves in front of Elan. Her golden eyes fix on him. "Can I pet her?"

"Of course."

Elan's gaze turns threatening, and he halts.

"Elan! Enough with your act already. I know you like the attention."

Her glare softens. *Oh, just a little bit.* She nudges Harut with her snout, keeping her nostrils upwind. *As long as his smell doesn't stick to me.* She flashes all her teeth in her intimidating smile.

"Elan!" I can't believe she's being so rude.

Harut chuckles. "She's a cheeky one, isn't she?" He rubs her nose. "Don't worry. My smell won't stick to you. I would have thought you would be used to the smell, seeing as you like dead animals and everything."

Elan throws her head back. *You take that back! I don't like dead animals. I like live animals. They don't stink, and the meat is fresh, not rotten.*

He throws his hands up in resignation. "Okay, okay. I get it. My bad."

The field starts to clear of Valkyries and angels of death, and the bodies of the wounded soldiers remain unmoving. A few soldiers wander through the bodies, searching for any survivors among the injured.

Mistress Sigrun lands not far from us, her face wearing the usual scowl that she reserves for my kind. "Wingless. It's time to go."

"I'll come back shortly, Mistress." It is an effort to not sound like a spiteful brat, but I do my best to keep my voice even.

"You need to come back now, wingless!"

Grr. She makes it so hard to be respectful. "My name is Kara, Mistress Sigrun! And I will come back when I'm ready. Right now, I'm talking to my friend."

She glowers at me and places her hands on her hips before she huffs then springs into the sky.

"You have such a friendly mistress," Harut says sarcastically.

"You don't have to tell me."

We watch the Valkyries disappear one by one.

"Harut!" a voice calls across the distance. "What are you doing? You're talking with the enemy." A scowling angel of death lands in front of us, his beautiful back wings spread with annoyance, making him seem more intimidating.

- CHAPTER NINE -

The angel of death is standing intimidatingly in front of me, his hand hovering over the hilt of his sheathed sword. "Harut, you shouldn't be this close to a Valkyrie. They are our enemies."

Harut blocks the angel of death's access to me. "Kara is not our enemy."

Two more angels of death land next to the first, soft thuds sounding as their feet touch the ground.

"Do you need assistance, Harut?" one of the new angels of death asks. "Are you unable to defeat this Valkyrie?" Sliding metal grinding against metal rings out as he draws his sword.

Harut remains in front of me. "Guys, I'm fine. Kara is not a normal Valkyrie."

Pulling from my inner strength, I stand next to Harut. There are too many angels of death for me to fight, although I know Elan would help. "I can't reap souls. You can relax. I am not your competition. Harut has witnessed that I'm unable to do it." I remove my coat and expose my back to strike out any suspicion. "And I don't have wings. I'm different. I'm not like the other Valkyries."

The angel of death on the other side of the first moves forward with his sword drawn. My left arm twitches as the magic courses through it. I can feel it swirling in my arm, all the way up to my head, waiting for my heart to instruct it.

As though something in my eyes is scaring him, the angel of death pauses, but he looks at me menacingly. The three of them don't seem convinced and look indecisive over what to do next.

Heavy footsteps sound behind me, and the ground quivers. I realize that Elan is visible and standing over us. By observing the hesitancy on the angels of death's faces, I know her expression is aggressive and showing she is ready to attack.

The first angel backs away slowly. "The battle is over, and it's time to go. Are you coming, Harut?" Without waiting for an answer, he pushes off into the sky, followed by the other two angels.

Trying to settle the magic down, I open and clench my fist several times.

"Well, I guess that's me." Harut clasps my upper arm, and again, the strange sensation of coldness mixed with warmth floods through my skin. It must be the coldness of death blended with his feelings toward me. "Perhaps I will see you again soon." His black eyes seem to see right through me, and heat rises to my cheeks again. I enjoy our friendship, although I also find it confusing when his handsome face looks at me that way.

I nod. "I guess I should be going, too, and see what happens when I get back to Asgard. It will be interesting to see if Mistress Sigrun honors her agreement, even though she's bitter about it."

His eyes travel up Elan. "Goodbye, dragon. It was nice to make your acquaintance."

I watch him fly off as gracefully as any of the Valkyries, and that familiar tug of envy over their glorious wings tears at me. I pull my cloak back on and turn to find Elan standing over me, watching Harut disappear.

You always have trouble wherever you go. Don't you, Kara? Never is a day boring around you. She smiles and shakes her head. *And who would have thought it would be like that? Here I was, thinking that to settle around you in Asgard, waiting for you to come and do something, would be mundane. But no, you manage to get into all the trouble you possibly can.*

I shrug and slide my hood over my head. "You're a dragon. I thought you liked a little excitement."

Living a life with you makes the dragon fields look like a mild place to live.

"What can I say? I want to do great things, and with that comes a lot of disruption in the world of Valkyries, and it looks like it is the same in the world of angels of death too."

Even though you are a complete handful, I don't mind. She nudges me with her nose. *I love an entertaining life.*

After petting her nose, I climb onto her back, hook my feet into the stirrups, and collect the reins. "I get it, Elan. I'm a handful. You'd be bored without me."

She looks at me over her shoulder and winks then jumps into the sky, heading back to our entry point near the forest. The rainbow bridge flashes expectantly in front of us, and we submit to its beckoning, allowing ourselves to be sucked into its vacuum. With a thump, we land on the solid ground of Asgard. Heimdall stands on guard in his usual position. His hand rests on the hilt of his sword, which is pointing at the ground.

"About time, young Valkyrie," he grumbles. "You've managed to annoy Mistress Sigrun again. That, I can tell."

"Pfft. What's new?" I wave a hand dismissively. "I have managed to do that many times. Seeing as no one came to grab me from Midgard, I'm guessing she said I had her permission to be there."

He shakes his head, and his brow furrows. "No. That was the strange thing, but she didn't say that you are no longer allowed to go and help with the battles."

"That's a nice change. I guess this is one step in the right direction."

Apprehensive, he stares at Elan. "That's some vicious-looking dragon you've got there."

"Not to me, she's not."

"But her kind is vicious. You're lucky to have her as a friend."

"I know. Together, we are going to make big changes."

Heimdall peers down at me. His eyes fill with humor, and a strange sound rumbles from his throat. A moment later, he holds his stomach and throws his head back, and a large cackle bursts from his mouth. "If you say so."

"Oh, I do, and I know I'm right. Anyway, see you next time." I look at Elan. "Let's get out of here."

As we fly over Asgard, I marvel at the difference in the scene from Midgard. Here, it is so gray and bare looking, a complete contrast to the greenness of Midgard. My arm begins to tingle again, but I ignore it, as it is becoming a part of my everyday life. Maybe the tingling is because the magic is growing within me.

Elan lands within walking distance of the academy. After removing the saddle, I throw it over my arm and top it with my cloak, then I stroke her nose with my free hand. "Thanks, Elan."

She nudges me, and I leave, pondering over another strange day and the disappointment that I can't reap souls for Valhalla. It must be in our blood that all wingless Valkyries cannot do this. Even so, I still want to be involved in the battle and prove that we are useful in other ways.

As I march back to the academy, something swoops behind me, and claws clasp my back and scratch through my leather clothes. I drop the saddle and cloak and scream in pain. I spin around to see the creature flying above me. It has attacked me from behind. This is weird.

I cry, "What are you doing? I've done nothing to you, Loki. Why are you attacking for no reason?"

The zmey sweeps down again, claws first, and I yank my sword out of its sheath on my back, blocking the attack. Pain sears my side, but I don't dare drop my sword as the zmey swoops down a couple more times. I wave the sword menacingly. If the book is right, this is Loki. But as I look into the creature's eyes, I don't see a similarity to any god. The creature looks completely vicious and aggressive.

I call again, "Loki, I know it's you. Stop! Change into your god form so we can talk about this."

As I wait in hope, the creature flies down and attacks again. I'm dumbfounded. It appears as though he is trying to kill me.

- CHAPTER TEN -

I'm ready to scream for Elan when the zmey swoops down one more time, but then the creature flies away. I watch it disappear into the distance, speechless over what it did. My back aches, and I explore the damage with my hands. When I pull them back, they're covered in my blood. Another scratch runs up my side, but it doesn't go as deep. Blood and rips have ruined my black leather clothes. My head tells me I should head to Anita in case the creature's claws are infected. Instead, I follow my heart and stash my saddle and cloak under a large rock and head in the opposite direction.

The magic of the dark elf is a pull that I can't resist. I wander into the narrow dark tunnel that leads to the dingy little cave buried deep within the mountain. Eventually, I reach the area with the lights and turn the corner. The distance doesn't seem as far as the last time. As luck would have it, the dark elf is sitting quietly in the corner with one of the large books sitting open on his lap. When he looks up at me, his eyes are filled with question, then he sees that I'm clutching my side with my bloodied hand.

"You need a healer, young Valkyrie."

"I can see the healer later. I'm fine."

"What happened?" He closes the book and places it on the pile.

"That's what I was coming to see you about. What do you know about Loki?"

A strange expression crosses his face, and his glowing yellow eyes seem to dim for a second. "Nothing other than he is a god and is quite mischievous. Why?"

"Because I read in the library that Loki is a zmey, like the one flying in the skies of Asgard. These marks are from a zmey. It attacked me without warning and wouldn't stop. I didn't even provoke it."

The dark elf's hairless eyebrows rise, and he stares at me. "Are you sure it was the creature that marks with magic? The one that marked you originally?" He rises to his feet and gestures to the injury. "May I see?"

I turn to expose my side to him and flinch when he touches the edges.

"It's not too deep. Let me apply some ointment." Gilroma grabs a container from the far corner, and it clinks against the other bottles as he pulls it out. His footsteps are slow as he approaches me while dipping his fingers into the solution. As he runs his hand over the wound, a strange sensation slowly courses through it from top to bottom. "That should do."

I twist to gaze at the spot but struggle to see it, so I reach around to feel it. It is healed, and I can't feel a mark like the one left on my shoulder. "Thanks," I say, confused yet not willing to question the complete recovery. "Why would the creature mark me again?"

The strange elf paces then stops and sits on a rock not far from me. His glowing eyes watch me intensely, then he speaks slowly, as though weighing his words. "I do not think this is a mark of aggression. I think this is a mark of magic. The only reason why I think the zmey has marked you again is because, for some reason, the creature wants your power to be stronger."

"What? I haven't worked out how to use the first lot of magic."

He nods slowly. "That will come with time and with more lessons from me. What you had served its purpose, and it wasn't a powerful form of magic."

"I thought it was powerful. It helped me against the winged Valkyries." I frown. "Why would it pick me?"

He shrugs. "You were marked once. Why not finish the job?"

"But it's not something I asked for. I only wanted to have wings and to be able to reap souls like the other Valkyries. None of those came to pass. This happened instead."

"You should be grateful for what you've been given." A strange dark shadow passes over his eyes. "You may find that many of the winged Valkyries will become envious of you."

"The main purpose of the Valkyrie is to reap souls. I can't reap them, so why would they be jealous?" I ask, arms flailing. "I just want to reap souls like a regular winged Valkyrie."

The dark elf sits against the wall and crosses his legs then his arms, leaning back. The leg that overhangs the other kicks back and forth a

few times as though he is deep in thought.
"You know, there is a reason why you can't
reap souls."

"Yeah, because I wasn't born with wings
and the blood of the Royal Valkyries." I don't
bother hiding the spite in my voice.

"Yes and no," he says hesitantly.

I stop pacing and look at him directly.
"What do you mean, 'no'?"

"The winged Valkyries can only reap souls
because Odin has blessed them."

I snap, "Yes, yes. When they are conceived,
they naturally have Odin's blessing because of
their wings."

The dark elf kicks the top leg some more,
and it irritates me. "Not exactly."

"What do you mean?" I ask again, more
sharply.

He stops kicking his leg and uncrosses it,
placing his foot on the floor. "Odin blesses
them with the power after they are born—once
he sees that they were born with wings. That is

why all of the winged Valkyries look almost identical. They change after they have been blessed."

I stop pacing and stare at him openmouthed. "Do you mean Odin purposely leaves out the wingless Valkyries?"

He nods. "Yes. But you're not a hopeless case. If you go to Odin and prove yourself, he may bless you with the gift as well. He has the power to grant this to a Valkyrie at any stage of their life."

I lean forward and hold my stomach, letting out a loud breath in the form of a sarcastic laugh. "As if that's going to happen. Odin hates me."

"No. Odin doesn't hate you. He despises the fact that you are bucking the system, going against his wishes and his dominance. He is a god who opposes change. You need to play into his ego a bit more and learn how to work him. Then he will be more likely to change."

"A difficult task, wouldn't you say?"

He nods. "Yes, it is difficult. But now I have told you what you need to do if that is what you really want. How you take it from here is up to you." He rises to his feet and clasps his hands behind his back. "Now. Let's see what this newfound magic can do."

The End

ACKNOWLEDGMENTS

I am touched by the enormous amount of support I have received from my immediate family. My husband has been a helpful first reader and at times been a wonderful motivator, with hints of ideas to help me through the blanks. The support from my three sons has also been overwhelming. They have put up with my head being in the clouds, thinking about the next plot twist or story for several years. Along with many hours spent working on my books and keeping in touch with my readers.

A big thank you to my extended family who support me being a book enthusiast.

A huge thank you to my editor, Susannah Driver, her editing and writing tips, and my Proofreader, Kristina B, for picking up the things we missed.

Thank you to all of my readers who have loved my work, and continue to read my stories. I would love for you to share your thoughts in a review on one or all of the following:

Amazon.com
Goodreads
Barnes & Noble
You can follow Katrina Cope at:

https://www.facebook.com/Author.Katrina.Cope

https://twitter.com/Katrina_R_Cope

https://www.goodreads.com/author/show/7265107.Katrina_Cope

https://www.katrinacopebooks.com

http://http://www.amazon.com/Katrina-Cope/e/B00F00JF9M/

Book 6 of Valkyrie Academy Dragon Alliance Series 'Ambushed' released November 2019.

BOOKS BY KATRINA COPE

~~~~~

Pre-Teen Books

THE SANCTUM SERIES

JAYDEN'S CYBERMOUNTAIN

SCARLET'S ESCAPE

TAYLOR'S PLIGHT

ERIC & THE BLACK AXES

ADRIANNA'S SURGE

~~~~~

Young Adult Urban Fantasy

AFTERLIFE SERIES

FLEDGLING

THE TAKING

ANGELIC RETRIBUTION

DIVIDED PATHS

Afterlife Novelette

THE GATEKEEPER

~~~~~

Young Adult Urban Paranormal Fantasy

SUPERNATURAL EVOLVEMENT SERIES

(Associated with the Afterlife Series)

WITCH'S LEGACY (#0.5 Prequel)

AALIYAH

~~~~~

Young Adult Fantasy Nordic Myths

VALKYRIE ACADEMY DRAGON ALLIANCE

SERIES

MARKED (Prequel)

CHOSEN

VANISHED

SCORNED

INFLICTED

EMPOWERED

AMBUSHED

WARNED

GET UPDATES & NOTIFICATIONS OF GIVEAWAYS

Would you like a FREE copy of Marked?
Visit here:
https://www.katrinacopebooks.com/valkyrie-academy-dragon-alliance
Through this link you can sign up for my newsletter and receive a FREE copy of Marked plus updates about my fantasy books, sales and notification of giveaways.

DID YOU ENJOY THIS BOOK?
YOU CAN MAKE A BIG DIFFERENCE.

Honest reviews of my books help bring them to the attention of other readers.

If you've enjoyed this book, I'd be grateful if you could spend a few minutes leaving a review (it can be as short as you like).
The review can be left on Amazon and Goodreads.
Thank you very much.

ABOUT THE AUTHOR

Katrina is an author of several Young Adult and Preteen/Middle Grade novels. Each of her released books reaching the top 100 in certain categories on the Amazon's Best Sellers Rank – a few even as high as number one.

She resides in Queensland, Australia. Her three teenage boys and husband for over nineteen years treat her like a princess. Unfortunately though, this princess still has to do domestic chores.

From a very young age, she has been a very creative person and has spent many years travelling the world and observing many different personalities and cultures. Her favourite personalities have been the strange ones, yet the ones under the radar also hold a place in her heart.

During her last extensive travels, she spent 16 nights in a bomb shelter on a Kibbutz 8 kilometers off the Lebanese border. It was to avoid Katyusha bombs that the resident volunteers decided to name her after (she is still trying to work out why).

Katrina's online home is at www.katrinacopebooks.com

You can connect with Katrina on:

Twitter https://twitter.com/Katrina_R_Cope

Facebook

https://www.facebook.com/Author.Katrina.Cope

Instagram

https://www.instagram.com/katrina_cope_author

Pinterest

https://www.pinterest.com.au/katrinacope56

Email authorkatrinacope@gmail.com